Other books by Walker & Company

The Period Book: Everything You Don't Want to Ask (But Need to Know)
by Karen and Jennifer Gravelle

What's Going On Down There? Answers to Questions Boys Find Hard to Ask
by Karen Gravelle, with Chava and Nick Castro

Girl Talk: Staying Strong, Feeling Good, Sticking Together
by Judith Harlan

Girl Thoughts: A Girl's Own Incredible, Powerful, and Absolutely Private Journal
by Judith Harlan

5 Ways to Know About You
by Karen Gravelle

The Boy's Book of Lists
by David P. Langston

The Best Friends' Handbook

The Totally Cool One-of-a-Kind Book About You and Your Best Friend

Erica Orloff & Alexa Milo

ILLUSTRATIONS BY Carolyn Fisher

FOR LAUREN..

Carolyn Fisher

Walker & Company ☀ New York

To our best friends —E. O. & A. M.

To my best friend, Steve —C. F.

Text copyright © 2002 by Erica Orloff and Alexa Milo
Illustrations copyright © 2002 by Carolyn Fisher

First published in the United States of America in 2002 by
Walker Publishing Company, Inc.

Published simultaneously in Canada by Fitzhenry and Whiteside, Markham, Ontario L3R 4T8

For information about permission to reproduce selections from this book, write to Permissions,
Walker & Company, 435 Hudson Street, New York, New York 10014

Library of Congress Cataloging-in-Publication Data

Orloff, Erica.
    The best friends' handbook: the totally cool one-of-a-kind book about you and your best friend/Erica Orloff &
Alexa Milo; illustrations by Carolyn Fisher.
        p. cm
    Summary: Suggests projects and writing exercises for celebrating friendship and documenting your relation-
ship with your best friend.
    ISBN 0-8027-7645-0 (paperback)
        1. Friendship—Juvenile literature. [1. Best friends. 2. Friendship.] I. Milo, Alexa. II. Fisher, Carolyn, 1968–, ill.
III. Title.

BJ1533.F8 O75 2002
177'.62—dc21

                                                                                                    2002066185

Carolyn Fisher created the illustrations using Corel Painter.

Book design by Sophie Ye Chin

Visit Walker & Company's Web site at www.walkerbooks.com

Printed in the United States of America

2   4   6   8   10   9   7   5   3   1

ACKNOWLEDGMENTS

We would like to thank our family: John (aka Dad), Nicholas, and Isabella, Grandma, and Pop, for believing in our book.

Alexa would like to thank all of her friends for being so excited about the book.

Erica would like to thank all her wonderful friends for being so special: Pam, Kathy L., Kathy J., Nancy ("Nana"), and Cleo. And a particular thanks to Meredith Krashes, her best friend when she was a kid. I will never forget our all-night Monopoly sessions and snoring dogs and all those silly and special memories.

CONTENTS

Introduction

Friendship is a very special gift. We all know that feeling when we find a friend who seems to understand us inside and out. A best friend knows us as well as we know ourselves—and sometimes better! Sometimes our friend can seem like our twin. Other friends can be very different from us, and that's what makes them so interesting. Either way, this book celebrates friendship—especially best friendship.

Do you have a best friend? Someone you can tell *anything* to? Isn't it great to know you have a special friend who accepts you just the way you are?

This book was born when Erica and Alexa decided to write a celebration of special friends. We hope you will share this book with your friends and especially your best friend. There are pages to fill in and journaling activities. When you are finished with this book, tuck it away in a safe place. Years from now you can take it out and recall these special times with a smile.

We wrote this book after Erica, Alexa's mom, watched Alexa and her best friends. Sometimes, it was almost as if they shared a secret language. She recognized those times when Alexa and her friends spent all weekend sleeping at each other's houses—only to call each other an hour after they parted to talk for hours on the phone. There were nights when Alexa and her best friend watched television together—via telephone—Alexa in her room, and her friend at her own house five miles away! Seeing Alexa and her best friends' silly, fun, and zany times brought back memories of Erica's own childhood best friend. She considers herself very lucky that she and her friend Meredith are still close today—after more than twenty years!

Though you may have one special best friend now, throughout your life you may end up with a few best friends. You might have a best friend from grade school, high school, then later on in college. You may have a best friend of the opposite sex—years from now you may even end up best friends with the very same sibling you fight with now! (You may be saying, "No way," but it happened to Erica.)

The most important point to remember is that having a best friend is about acceptance and love, about being yourself and seeing each other through good times and bad. So read on and have fun with your very best friend.

You and Your Best Friend: A Story

CHAPTER ONE

A ring is round, it has no end,
and that's how long we'll be best friends.

—childhood rhyme

This chapter is about you and your best friend. How did you meet? What do you like most about each other? What do you have in common? How are you different? Do you have a "secret language"?

Erica recalls when she and her best friend used to draw bubbles all over their notes to each other in junior high school, symbolizing their first teenage loves. You know, like the bubbles you blow out of a bottle with a wand? Well, somehow they thought that was what love was like, so they used to draw them on notes they passed each other in class.

Alexa and her best friend used an expression—"VERY INNNNNNTTER-ESSSSSSSSSTING"—for certain moments, but they can't explain exactly why they said it or even who was the first one to come up with it. That's what's special about best friends—sharing secrets, goofy songs and stories, and special phrases with each other. And most important, these songs, jokes, and phrases mean something only to the two of you!

This chapter is where you write about all the unique elements of your friendship. Ideally, you and your best friend will each have a book in which you will write about your friendship. You can complete sections when you're apart and then compare them, or you can fill them out together the next time you have a sleepover.

There are no right or wrong answers to any of these questions. This is all about sharing one-of-a-kind memories, secrets, and fun. Feel free to doodle on these pages. These memories are yours—as original and different as each friendship.

One more note: There's no rule stating that your best friend must be a girl (if you're a girl) or must be a boy (if you're a boy). Either way, fill out this journaling chapter about you and your best friend—and most important, have fun!

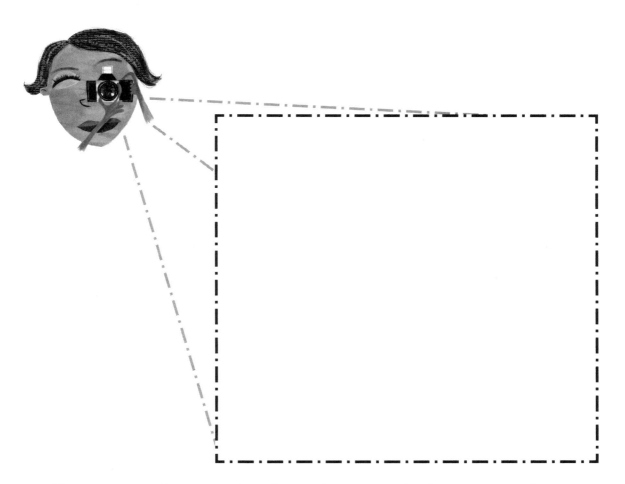

This is a picture of me and my best friend taken on (describe the day or write the date):

_____

_____

ABOUT MY BEST FRIEND

My best friend's name is _Danielle Blankestijn_

We met (describe when, where, and how you met) We met at awana are mom stard to talk and me and Danielle and I said hi and began to talk we have now nowen ecber for 2 years now we are best friend's!

What I like most about my best friend is funny she has great ideas she is kind she is great fashanabel

The ways my best friend is different from me are _____

_____

_____

_____

_____

The ways my best friend is the same as I am are _____

_____

_____

_____

_____

The five adjectives that best describe my best friend are

1. _____

2. _____

3. _____

4. _____

5. _____

ABOUT OUR FRIENDSHIP

The funniest thing that ever happened to my best friend and me was when

_____

_____

_____

_____

_____

_____

We have been through some difficult times, too. The hardest thing my best friend ever helped me face was when _____

_____

_____

_____

_____

_____

It's a Friday night. You'll catch us doing this together:

_____

_____

_____

_____

_____

_____

_____

_____

ARGH! An argument . . . the one thing we agree to disagree on is _____

_____

_____

_____

_____

_____

_____

Our friendship is most like

1. Lucy and Ethel on <u>I Love Lucy</u>. We get into ridiculous and very funny situations together.

2. Harry Potter and Hermione Granger. We may bicker sometimes, but we really couldn't be closer.

3. Gilligan and Skipper on <u>Gilligan's Island</u>. One of us is always getting us into trouble, but the Skipper keeps an eye on Gilligan to make sure we're really OK.

4. Shaggy and Scooby. We think, EAT, and act exactly alike.

5. Tom and Jerry. We fight like cats and dogs . . . or cats and mice?

The most fun we ever had together was when we _____

_____

_____

_____

_____

_____

The most embarrassing thing that ever happened to us was when _____

_____

_____

_____

_____

One silly thing about us that no one knows is _____

_____

_____

_____

_____

If our friendship had a theme song, it would be (and why) _____

_____

_____

_____

_____

_____

_____

_____

Don't tell anyone . . . the most trouble we ever got into together was when

_____

_____

_____

_____

_____

_____

_____

Hollywood is calling! Movie producers have just called, and they're making a blockbuster about our friendship. Who will play each of us? And what kind of movie will it be?_____

_____

_____

_____

_____

_____

Our favorite expressions are _____

_____

_____

_____

_____

We have to choose a mascot to represent us. What pair of
animals would best define our friendship? _____

_____

_____

_____

_____

Aliens from another planet have just kidnapped us. We're going to frighten
them into freeing us by being *very weird*. What we do is this: _____

_____

_____

_____

_____

Our favorite slumber party snacks are _____

_____

_____

_____

_____

_____

_____

Help! We're stranded on a desert island. We can bring only five things to tide us over until we're rescued. What five things would we bring?

1. _____

2. _____

3. _____

4. _____

5. _____

This space is for *your best friend* to write anything he or she wants to about
your friendship. _____

_____

_____

_____

_____

_____

_____

_____

_____

_____

_____

_____

_____

_____

_____

_____

_____

_____

_____

We have to design a poster that is all about us. Here is our masterpiece.

your BF2

Best Friend Quotient

CHAPTER TWO

A true friend is the best possession.
—Benjamin Franklin, U.S. statesman,
author, inventor, printer, publisher, and all-around smart guy

Are you ready for a challenge? Take our best friend test. Tease your brain. Exercise your mind muscle. Just how much do you know about your best friend?

How to take this quiz? It's easy. You and your best friend answer all the questions asked about each other. If you each have a book, your best friend fills out all the answers about you in his or her book, and you fill out all the answers about him or her in yours. If not, you can always photocopy these pages, or write your answers on a separate sheet of paper. It's up to you.

No cheating now! Then, you pop a big bowl of popcorn and start answering questions. See who got the most answers right. Then look at our BFQ scores (like an IQ score) to see just how well you know your best friend. But remember, half the fun is finding out the answers to all these really riveting questions about your best friend!

1. Where was your best friend born?

_____

2. What is your best friend's middle name?

_____

3. Has your best friend had his or her tonsils out?

_____

4. Has your best friend ever broken a bone?

_____

5. No peeking! . . . Does your best friend wear a watch every day?

_____

6. Has your best friend ever had surgery other than a tonsillectomy?

_____

7. Has your best friend ever been sailing?

_____

8. Has your best friend ever traveled to a foreign country?

_____

9. What would your best friend say was his or her most amazing vacation?_____

_____

10. No peeking! . . . Does your best friend have pierced ears?

_____

☆ Bonus point if your best friend does and you know how old your best friend was when he or she got it done.

_____

11. Not counting pony rides, has your best friend ever ridden a horse?

_____

12 Does your best friend remember his or her dreams after waking up?
_____

13 Can your best friend do a cartwheel?
_____

14 What kind of toothpaste does your best friend use?
_____

15 What is the most embarrassing thing that ever happened to your best friend? _____
_____
_____

16 What is your best friend's all-time favorite food?
_____

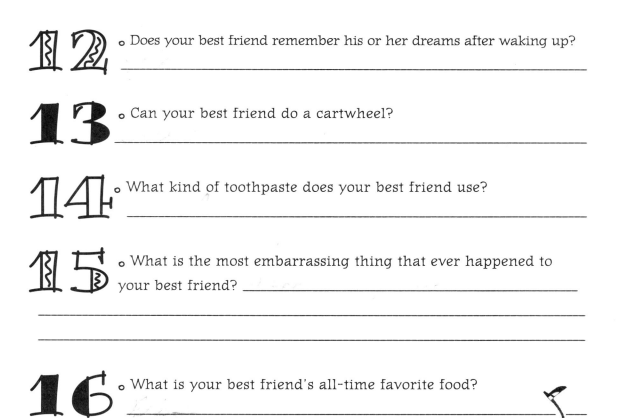

17 ○ What is your best friend's favorite candy?

_____

18 ○ You are baking your best friend his or her most favorite
birthday cake. What kind is it? _____

_____

19 ○ What is your best friend's favorite flavor of Jell-O?

_____

20 ○ What is your best friend's favorite flavor of ice cream?

_____

☆ Bonus point if you know what his or her favorite topping is.

_____

21 ○ What is your best friend's favorite beverage?

_____

22. What is your best friend's favorite vegetable?

_____

 23. Ketchup or mustard on your best friend's hot dog?

_____

24. Which of the following statements most accurateley defines your best friend's attitude toward chocolate?

        (a.) "It is a life-sustaining force and I cannot live without it!"

        (b.) "I can take it or leave it. But don't let me be without

                my potato chips!"

        (c.) "Chocolate? I'd rather eat worms!"

25. When it comes to "Got Milk?" how does your best friend feel?

        (a.) Chocolate milk

        (b.) Strawberry-flavored

        (c.) Plain

        (d.) "YUCK!!! Milk?!?!"

26. Is your best friend an adventurous eater?

> (a.) "Yes . . . my best friend would try roasted eel on toast!"
>
> (b.) "Somewhat . . . my best friend will try foods from different countries or new things on occasion."
>
> (c.) "No. Give my friend a burger and fries three hundred sixty-five days a year!"

27. Pancakes for breakfast. Does your best friend

> (a.) pour syrup all over the pancakes?
>
> (b.) pour syrup in one section and "dip"?
>
> (c.) go without?

28. Same scenario with french fries. Does your best friend

> (a.) pour ketchup over all the fries?
>
> (b.) "dip and dunk"?
>
> (c.) hate ketchup?

29. Lunchtime! Does your best friend

> (a.) make his or her own lunch?
>
> (b.) have Mom still pack it every day?
>
> (c.) buy his or her lunch?

30. Pizza time! What is your best friend's favorite pizza topping, or does your best friend like it plain?

Topings _____

☆ Bonus point if you have ever eaten an entire pie together!

_____

31. What is your best friend's most prized possession?
_____

32. What is your best friend's favorite holiday?
_____

33. What is your best friend's favorite article of clothing?
_____

34. What is your best friend's favorite color?
_____

35. What is your best friend's favorite animal?

cat

36. What is your best friend's favorite season of the year?

_____

37. What is your best friend's favorite restaurant?

_____

38. Does your best friend like gold or silver jewelry?

gold

39. Does your best friend like the great outdoors, like hiking and camping? Or does your best friend prefer the city?

_____

40. Does your best friend prefer baths or showers?

☆ Bonus point if you know your best friend's shampoo brand.

---

41. Science class. Time to dissect a frog. Would your best friend
- (a.) lead the experiment because he or she is so fascinated by science?
- (b.) watch through squinted eyes?
- (c.) organize a protest against the school for allowing animals to be dissected?

42. Your best friend has a choice of classes. Which does he or she pick?
- (a.) Art
- (b.) Shop/woodworking
- (c.) Home economics

 **43.** It's time to give an oral report in school. Your best friend

    (a.) *is in a panic. My best friend HATES talking in front of the class.*

    ✓ (b.) *isn't too worried. My best friend has worked hard on this report and knows it will go OK.*

    (c.) *can't WAIT! My best friend LOVES being the center of attention.*

44. Two-four-six-eight, go team!! Your best friend feels this way about cheerleading:

    (a.) *"Sign me up! I would love to be one."*

    (b.) *"Cheerlead? No way! They should cheer for ME while I play sports!"*

    ✓ (c.) *"Cheerlead? Play sports? Yuk!"*

45. What is your best friend's favorite sport to participate in?

_____

46. Gym class. Does your best friend love it or hate it?

_____

47. Does your best friend like math?

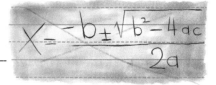

$$x = \frac{-b \pm \sqrt{b^2 - 4ac}}{2a}$$

_____

48. Who is, or was, your best friend's all-time favorite teacher?

_____

49. What one person annoys your best friend the most?

_____

50. Did your best friend have a "boyfriend" or "girlfriend" in kindergarten?

_____

☆ Bonus point if you know his or her kindergarten love's name.

_____

51. What is your best friend's favorite book?
Fudge

52. Who is your best friend's favorite actor?
Scarlet Joehasen

53. Who is your best friend's favorite actress?
Mathew Meconedy?

54. Who is your best friend's favorite cartoon character?
snoopy and minions

55. What is your best friend's favorite movie?
Winter solger

56. What is your best friend's favorite TV show?
Osccers Duesiz

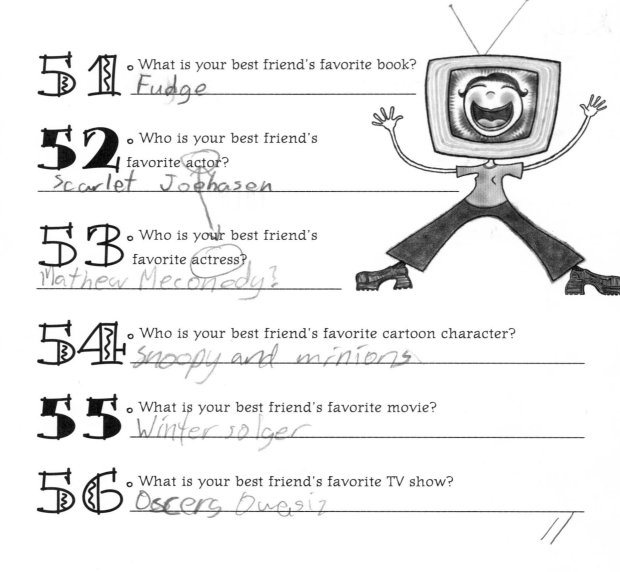

Rayne

57. Would your best friend like to be an actor or actress?

Actress

58. What is the scariest movie your best friend ever saw?

zootopia

59. Which is more important to your best friend?

(a.) His or her book collection.

(b.) His or her CD collection.

60. Who is your best friend's favorite singer or musical group?

newsboys / Jorden Flisce / Lindsey Sterling

☆ Bonus point if you've ever sung their songs at the top of your lungs together!

yes

61. Does your best friend believe in UFOs?

_NO !_

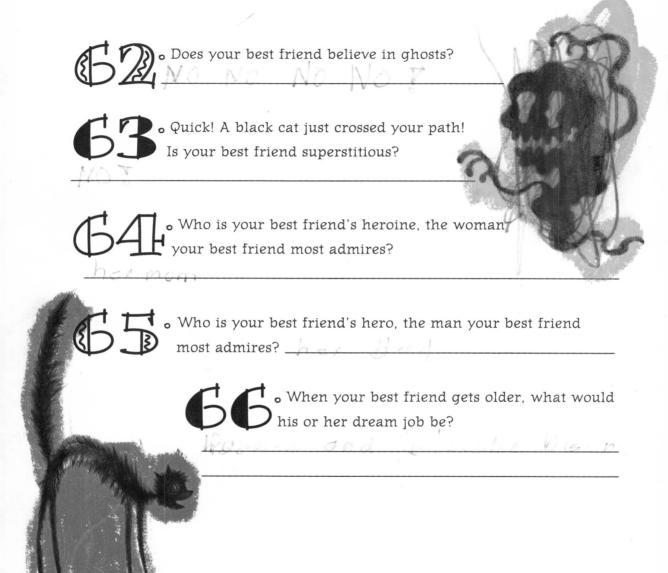

62. Does your best friend believe in ghosts?

_NO NO NO NO ?_

63. Quick! A black cat just crossed your path! Is your best friend superstitious?

_NO ?_

64. Who is your best friend's heroine, the woman your best friend most admires?

her mom

65. Who is your best friend's hero, the man your best friend most admires? _her dad_

66. When your best friend gets older, what would his or her dream job be?

_____

67. Does your best friend believe in astrology?

_____

☆ Bonus point if you know your best friend's sign.

_____

68. How does your best friend feel about spiders?

    (a.) Runs screaming from the room.

    (b.) Stomps on it without a second thought.

    (c.) Catches it and releases it outside, poor baby.

69. Is your best friend afraid of the dark?

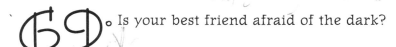

_____

70. Is your best friend afraid of mice, hamsters, and other furry little rodents? _____

71. Does your best friend chew gum?

      (a.) Constantly! *And blows bubbles, too!*

      (b.) Sometimes . . .

      (c.) Never.

72. Does your best friend have any nervous habits, such as twirling his or her hair or biting his or her nails?

_____

73. Does your best friend keep a journal?

_____

74. Does your best friend collect anything?

_____

75. Does your best friend wear perfume or cologne?

_____

76. When you have a sleepover, who is usually the first to fall asleep? _____

77. When you have a sleepover, who is usually the first to wake up? _____

78. Does your best friend sleep with one pillow or two? Or more?! _____

79. Does your best friend sleep with a nightlight? _____

80. Does your best friend sleep with a stuffed animal? _____

☆ Bonus point if your best friend does and you know its name!

_____

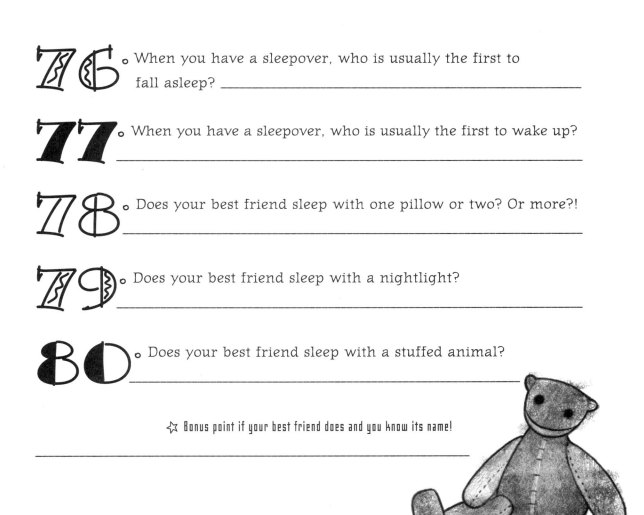

81. Does your best friend like to ham it up for the camera or is your best friend camera shy? _____
_____

82. If your best friend could have any pet in the entire world, what would he or she have? _____

_____

83. If your best friend wants to do something he or she doesn't think Mom or Dad will agree to, like see a PG-13 (or R-rated!) movie or go to a boy-girl party, who does your best friend ask first to try to get them on his or her side? _____

84. At the mall, what's the first store your friend wants to visit?
_____

85. Does your best friend usually fall asleep with TV or music on, or does your best friend need to have silence?

_____

86. What is your best friend's favorite expression?

_____

87. If your best friend could redecorate his or her room any way he or she wanted to, what would your best friend do to it?

_____

_____

88. Would your best friend ever call someone he or she had a crush on? _____

89. Your best friend has just been given $500 to spend in any way he or she wants. What does your best friend do with the money?

_____

_____

**.** Your best friend feels this way about clothes:

    (a.) "I have to have the absolute coolest, latest styles!"

    (b.) "I have a few favorite 'hot' outfits, but pretty much like
        to be comfortable and casual."

    (c.) "Clothes? Who cares? I grab whatever's clean and in my closet."

☆ Bonus point if your best friend has ever loaned you an article of clothing because you absolutely loved it!

. Would your best friend ever like to try skydiving?

_____

. Camping in the woods or a fancy hotel? What is your best
friend's idea of a dream vacation?

---

93. What is the ONE thing your best friend does that drives his
or her parents crazy? _____

---

94. In your best friend's family, including grandparents, brothers and sisters, and parents, who is your best friend closest to? _____

95. How does your best friend feel about recycling?
   (a.) It's a pain.
   (b.) Doesn't give it much thought.
   (c.) It's so important to the environment!

96. It's eight o'clock in the morning. The sun is shining. The birds are chirping. It's the weekend. Your best friend's mother has just walked into his or her bedroom to say, "Come on, dear, time to eat breakfast and plan our day." Would your best friend
   (a.) hide beneath the pillow, shrieking, "What?!?!? I'm not supposed to get up for another five hours?!?!"
   (b.) be sitting on his or her bed, saying, "No problem, Mom, I've been up since six-thirty, anyway."
   (c.) ignore her completely and hope she'll go away?

97. Your best friend is having the worst hair day ever. What does your best friend do?

> (a.) Wear a hat.
>
> (b.) Put it in a ponytail, if it's long enough, or add a LOT of gel.
>
> (c.) Put a pillow over his or her head and refuse to come out of the bedroom.

98. The roller coaster has got three loop-de-loops! Does your best friend say

> (a.) "No way, let's find the merry-go-round."
>
> (b.) "The more upside-down loops the better!"

99. Does your best friend cry at sad movies?

> (a.) Never.
>
> (b.) Sometimes.
>
> (c.) We can't go unless we bring an entire box of tissues!

100.

If your best friend's parents let your best friend keep his or her room any way that your best friend wanted, how would his or her bedroom be?

(a.) So clean you could eat off the floor.

(b.) There's a science experiment growing under my best friend's bed!

(c.) Something in between.

☆ Bonus point if you know for a fact there really is a science experiment growing under your best friend's bed.

SCORING

Each correctly answered question and bonus question is worth one point. Add up both your scores and then divide by two to get your best friend know-it-all score.

1 POINT TO 40 POINTS: We call you Discoverers. Okay, so you don't know everything about your best friend. That's what makes friendship so interesting. You keep getting to discover new fun facts about each other. Congratulations! You and your best friend now know more trivia about each other because you took this test.

41 POINTS TO 60 POINTS: We call you Half-and-Halfs. You answered about half the questions right, and we admit, some of them weren't easy. You know quite a bit about your best friend. Great job!

61 POINTS TO 80 POINTS: You're best friend Aces. You got more than half the questions right, and you definitely know a lot about your best friend. You may even know more about those little details than anyone else on the planet!

81 POINTS TO 100 POINTS: You're best friend Champs. You know just about everything there is to know about your best friend. But remember, the fun is in finding out still new, funny, and exciting things about each other and in having endless adventures and memories together. Great going, Champs!

100 POINTS TO 110 POINTS: There were ten bonus points in there (if you were counting), so if you scored greater than 100 points, we're calling you best friend Super-Geniuses! WOW! And we thought no one could get all 100. If you did, write us care of our publisher and we promise to write you back with a gold star of friendship! Great going, Super-Geniuses!!!

CHAPTER THREE

Friendship Time Capsule

Friendship is the only cement that will ever hold the world together.
—Woodrow Wilson, 28th U.S. president

As much as you would love to remember everything about all the good times you and your best friend are sharing, you won't. Someday, you will both be grown up, with careers, maybe families, or you'll be off at college or traveling the world—wherever your dreams may take you. But these experiences, these memories you're making now, are worth keeping close to your heart forever. Maybe the two of you will still be best friends. We hope so. But even if time and circumstances take you away from each other, you can create a time capsule of memories to capture these moments. And if you are still the best of friends, you can open these capsules one day in the future and laugh together over all the old times.

This time capsule is a container in which you pack away all sorts of items that represent special memories. The capsule is meant to be opened at a later date—a much later date. The idea isn't to open it one year from now, or even five years from now. The idea is to open it ten or twenty or thirty years from now and enjoy the memories. Our capsule is easy to prepare. You will be making one for each of you. Just follow each step, and remember . . . have fun!

STEP ONE:

First of all, you need a container. You want it big enough to be able to put in notes and memories—movie tickets or photos or whatever has meaning for the two of you. But you don't want it SO big that lugging it around for the next decade or two will be a real pain in the neck. You also want something that you can seal shut so you're not tempted to peek in or reopen it once it is closed.

The following are some suggestions for a time capsule container:

- an empty coffee can
- a shoe box
- a manuscript box (you can buy these inexpensively at most office supply stores)
- a cigar box

You might even be able to find other more unusual containers, such as an old hatbox.

STEP TWO:

Next you want to decorate the outside of your capsule. This is limited only by your imagination. The best thing to use is a craft glue that will allow you to glue anything, from wood to pictures to cloth, on the outside of your capsule.

You want your decorations on the outside to be as fun as what is going to go inside of your capsule. Here are some things you might want to glue on:

- Photos of the two of you
- Movie ticket stubs
- Postcards from places you have visited together. The next time you go to a museum together or even a restaurant or amusement park that sells postcards, buy a couple; not to mail, but for your time capsule!
- Labels from favorite foods—can't live without a certain cereal or candy? What about a brand of macaroni and cheese, or soft drink or pizza? Whatever it is, if you eat it all the time and can't live without it, cut out a label and glue it on!
- "Dollars" or flat pieces from your favorite game. Of course,

if you can't play the game without it, then simply photocopy it, but if you can spare a Monopoly dollar or piece from your favorite board game, add it on.

- Your own artwork—if you're the supercreative sort, you can decorate your capsule with your own drawings and writings. Maybe even write a poem for the outside.
- Magazine pictures and cutouts of all your favorite stars, rock groups, even clothes and other style-related items. Erica says, "Trust me, you will smile twenty years from now at the clothes and fashion and hip music stars—especially when some of them turn out to be not so hip in the future. But who cares—you love them NOW!"

☆ A little hint: If you use something like a coffee can, cover it with white acrylic paint, which will be a better background to glue on all these other items.

Remember, you are both decorating a capsule so that you each will have one. You should do this activity together so that you have input on each other's capsule. The idea is that the capsule should reflect a bit of both of you.

Photo Fun

Here are some tips about taking photos for both the inside and outside of your capsule.

- You should have at least one photo of the two of you that reflects you looking your best.
- You should have some "action photos"—photos showing the two of you doing some of your favorite activities, like cycling at the park, in-line skating, or listening to music with a hundred CDs spread all around you.
- You should include group photos that show your other friends.
- Try to have some personal shots that reflect "the real you" for both of you. For instance, if you totally adore your dog or cat, then snap a picture of you with your pet. You'll want memories of all the aspects of your friendship and life. If you are an accomplished musician or athlete, and you'd like your friend to remember that about you, get pictures reflecting those traits.
- Take some totally, ridiculously silly pictures. Pictures with hats, sunglasses, wacky clothes or makeup . . . anything goofy that still reflects your friendship.
- Include some everyday pictures from school. If you're

worried about taking an expensive camera to school, take a disposable one instead.

Remember, the idea is to capture the "essence" of you and your friendship. Best of all, the pictures should show you laughing and smiling—the glowing look of having fun as only you two can experience!

STEP THREE:

FILL UP YOUR TIME CAPSULE

Once the outside of your time capsule is completed, it's time to fill the inside. You can include more of the same things as on the outside. You can also include bulkier items that wouldn't glue on the outside of your capsule. Here are some suggestions:

- Souvenir trinkets and key chains from places you've visited or from activities you like to do together.
- Pressed flowers or corsages from dances you went to as double dates.
- Brochures from amusement parks and other sites or field trips you went to together.
- Playbills from plays you went to, or concert or baseball programs.

- Cards or letters you have written to each other.
- Try to include at least one "class note" from notes you passed to each other in school.
- More pictures and magazine shots of people and things you like.

Now we have two tasks for you. One is to include a present. You should each go out and buy the other a small gift. Try to limit it to something under five dollars. The idea isn't that this is something expensive but that it expresses your friendship. (Remember, too, that it has to fit in the capsule!) Wrap the gift, and place it in your best friend's capsule.

Your next task is to write your best friend a letter. Remember, she or he isn't going to open this for a long, long time. You might write about where you would both like to be in the future. Write about silly things from right now, about memories, about how much your best friend means to you. Place that in each other's time capsule.

But don't seal your capsules yet. There's one last thing to include. . . .

THE PROMISE

After your time capsules are decorated and filled up, you have to decide when you are going to open them. Set a date you'll remember. January first would be a good idea. Then set the year. Try to set a date that will be after you both get out of college or are settled into careers for a little bit. For instance, if both of you are twelve or thirteen, you would want to set the date for at least twelve years from now. Write the date on a seal—"Do not open until . . ."—that you put on top.

     Next, you each need to write the following pledge on a slip of paper and put it in each other's capsule:

I, _____ (fill in your name), **do solemnly swear** that I will NOT open this capsule before _____ (fill in your chosen date). I also solemnly swear that if my best friend and I have lost touch, I will attempt to track her down and call her within one week of opening this capsule. At that time, we will remember all these good times. I also solemnly swear to look back on these times with a happy heart and remember the fun!

SIGNED,

_____
(And sign your name)

Now you're ready for the final step.

STEP FOUR:

Have a small ceremony to seal your capsules. Close them up and tape them shut. Tie a ribbon around your capsule that will be cut the day you open it—and not a day sooner! Then place your capsule on the tippy-top shelf of your closet or some other place where you will *almost* forget about it for a long time—probably until you move out on your own and your mom tells you to get all the junk out of your old closet!

One more important point: Tell your mom or dad that you have done this so they don't find this capsule someday and accidentally throw it out. Tell them how important it is.

You've done it! Congratulations! You've created your own friendship time capsule!

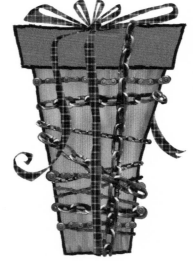

CHAPTER FOUR

The BEST Best Friend ADVICE

Friends are the flowers in the garden of life.
—Author unknown

We would all love it if nothing ever went wrong between us and our best friend. Can things always stay the same? Can you and your best friend stay friends forever?

Erica has been close with her best friend from junior high school for more than twenty years now. She asked Meredith to recall some funny memories:

We'd be together in classes on and off all day at school and then go home and talk on the phone for as long as our parents would let us, every day! A lot of this schmoozing was most definitely about boys.

And . . .

We hung around together so much that people associated us as a pair and actually, more than once, we were accidentally called, "Eredith and Merica," which we found hilarious and would use to sign our many secret notes in class to each other. These notes also had lots of drawings of bubbles, which signified our "happiness."

Meredith now lives in New York and has traveled the world, sometimes even living in foreign countries for more than a year at a time. And yet, when she and Erica get together, it is as if no time has gone by, and they pick up where they left off. No, it's not the same as a "best friend" you see and talk to every day, but friendships grow and change.

Sadly, sometimes friendships do end. This can make you cry, lose sleep, or even feel sick to your stomach! Sometimes *you* are the one who wants a new best friend, but it doesn't feel very good knowing you are hurting your old best friend. The important thing to remember even during a fight is to try to treat your friend the way you would want to be treated.

Best friendships are . . . well, the best! But we also wanted to compile a list of questions about issues that best friends often face. Following each question are two sets of answers and advice. One answer is from Alexa, a kid just like you. The other answer is from Erica, a mom and an adult . . . but also someone who STILL has best friends she laughs with every day.

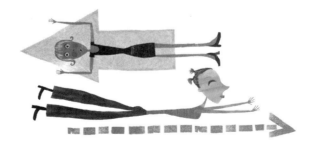

QUESTION: *My best friend and I have been friends for a while, but she is starting to hang out with another girl more than with me, and I don't think we will be best friends much longer. What should I do?*

Alexa's Advice: Start hanging out with other kids, too. You can't just have ONLY one friend. You and your best friend can still be close, but when you have other friends as well, you won't feel as bad if the two of you start to come apart.

Erica's Advice: Alexa has the right idea. There's nothing worse than feeling as if you and your very best friend are growing apart. But growing pains, I hate to say it, are part of getting older. Sometimes it feels terrible, but things usually work out for the best in the end.

By being friends with other kids, you can be sure that if things take a turn for the worse with your best friend, you still will have other girls and boys to call and hang around with. It would still hurt if your friendship ended or changed very much, but at least you wouldn't feel totally alone. And just because your best friend wants to be good friends with others, too, doesn't mean you will automatically be left out in the cold. Very often there's a way for you ALL to be friends. You'll find, over time, that life goes on, and a lost friendship doesn't hurt so much after a while. In the meantime, don't forget how terrific and neat and unique you are. Anyone would be lucky to have you as a friend or best friend.

QUESTION: *I just got in a fight with my friend. I really like her, but she is still mad at me. What can I do?*

Alexa's Advice: Tell her how you feel. I know it is probably easier said than done, but if you want to be friends you have to talk to her. You have to share your feelings—that's what true friendship is about.

Erica's Advice: Fights . . . ARGH! We hate having them, but they happen to all of us from time to time. The best solution to this is to avoid fights in the first place by remembering to communicate openly with your best friend.

Need an example? Okay . . . your best friend is always borrowing your favorite sweater, and she is always forgetting to return it, or when she does return it, it looks terrible, as if she hasn't taken care of it. Accidents happen, but this is the hundredth time she has done something like this. So you scream at her, "Why are you so careless with my things? You are so spoiled!" (Or something like that—which isn't the best way to communicate.)

Does that sound at all familiar? Imagine if the first time or second time your friend was careless with your things you had spoken up and said, "You know, I never mind loaning you my sweater, but please be more careful with it because I like it a lot and don't want it ruined. Thanks!" (And remember to smile.) What would happen? Your friend would know she was doing something that upset you, before it turned into a "big deal."

All right, so that's all great advice, but what if it's too late? What if, like in the question, you've already had the blowup? There are a few rules to fighting:

Fight fair. No name-calling, no being intentionally hurtful. If you haven't fought fair, you may not like it but you need to apologize—even if you feel you are the one owed an apology. Be the bigger person (which just means, be willing to be nice first).

You don't have to be right. No one does. Sometimes we are so busy fighting that we forget what it is we're fighting about. But in the end, it isn't all that important to be "right."

Along with the previous rules, remember what *is* important—and that's your friendship. Your friend should always be more important than an unkind word said when neither of you was thinking clearly. If it's hard to remember this, think about one of your favorite friendship memories, take a deep breath, and count to twenty—slowly—and try to calm down. Hey! This is your best friend, after all.

QUESTION: *There is this girl who used to be my best friend. She still thinks we are best friends. I don't want to hurt her feelings. What should I tell her?*

Alexa's Advice: That's a tough one. I think, though, you have to stop and look at why you aren't best friends. If you are really sure you don't want to be "best friends forever" (BFFs), then tell her. Be nice about it, though.

Erica's Advice: I sure like Alexa's last sentence. It is so difficult when we have to be honest with someone, and we know it's going to hurt them. It's almost as bad—or worse—than the situation being the other way around. Imagining what it would be like to have it happen to you can be helpful.

I also agree that it's important to be honest. Your former best friend needs to go find her own new best friend, someone she can share with and have good times with.

Remember, the title "best friend" is an honor. But even if you don't want to be "best friends" with someone, being a "really good friend" isn't too bad. Maybe that's the way you want to handle it.

QUESTION: *I like my best friend, but she just moved away to a new state. How can we keep our friendship going?*

Alexa's Advice: Be pen pals. Write letters back and forth. If you both have access to the Internet you can send E-mail or you can IM (Instant Message) each other. She'll start making other friends and so will you, and you have to face the fact that your relationship will have to adapt. It doesn't mean you can't keep on being friends.

Erica's Advice: Hurray for the computer! Between E-mail and Instant Messaging, you can feel as if your old friend is still right in your same town. I have more than a hundred E-mail addresses in my computer address book. Some addresses are for my business—being an author. But plenty of them are for friends from all the different times of my life. I have friends from junior high and high school whom I e-mail, friends from college, a couple of women I was roommates with after college. I have friends who were in writers groups with me (groups where you get together and work on your creative writing) when I was only twenty-two years old. I have friends from my first job, and friends from when Alexa was just born. Not only that, I still e-mail my four or five current best friends, even though we see each other at least once a week and talk on the telephone nearly every day!

If you don't have a computer, the telephone and snail mail are still great ways to keep in touch. And here's another idea if you don't have a computer: Tape messages to each other on audiotape or videocassette (or burn a CD if you're *really* technologically advanced!). I used to do this with Meredith

while I was in college. We would exchange them in the mail, and I would play these long (half hour or more) messages from her telling me about the latest people she was meeting, classes she was taking, and boys she was dating. I felt a little less homesick, or "friendsick," when I got to hear her voice.

QUESTION: *I don't have a best friend, and there is a girl in my class who seems really nice. I'm a bit nervous to ask her if we can be friends. Any suggestions about not being so nervous?*

Alexa's Advice: Be optimistic. Stop looking at all the bad things that can happen and start looking at the good things that can happen. Maybe she is just waiting for someone like you to come along!

Erica's Advice: At some periods in our lives, we can feel as if we are the only one without a best friend. That can be a lonely feeling, but like Alexa said, sometimes the person we want to be friends with is just as lonely as we are. Sometimes the other person is just waiting for us to take that first step. Friendship is something that can start out slowly. I'd say your first step is to make conversation. Remember to smile a lot. You can ask if this person might want to sit with you at lunch. Little by little, a real friendship can grow. If it works out, that's terrific. If it doesn't, you know what? You will still have gotten to know someone new!

QUESTION: *My best friend just started smoking. I tried to talk her out of it, but it didn't work, and now she is trying to get me to smoke. What do I tell her?*

Alexa's Advice: Tell her no! Smoking can really hurt you, and you do not want that to happen. Try to tell your friend that she should talk to her parents about what she is doing.

Erica's Advice: This is one of the hardest things about being good friends with someone. This question also relates to trying alcohol or drugs (though nicotine *is* a drug!); dieting too much or bingeing on food (or any other eating disorder); experimenting sexually more than he or she should at his or her age; or doing anything that is not healthy or happy for himself or herself. The problem is that part of being a best friend is swearing not to tell each other's secrets. This creates quite a dilemma.

    The best way to avoid this kind of problem has two parts:

1. Before either of you ever gets involved in something as harmful as smoking, you should promise each other to discuss it first. It should be a pact to make sure you both stay away from things that will ruin your health or bring unhappiness to you. This may not mean you can keep a friend from doing unhealthy things, but sometimes all a friend needs is a reminder of his or her goals for the future and some support to stay away from negative influences.

2. You should also make a pact with each other that if either of you tries something like this and finds that you can't stop, the other person can talk to a parent, teacher, counselor, or adult friend who can perhaps help.

I know both of these things sound a little unrealistic, and you might be thinking, "I could never tell on a friend," so that's why honesty and open communication are important. We hope you won't ever need to tell a parent or counselor because you have the kind of friendship that can withstand telling each other when the other person is about to do something unhealthy or dangerous. A real friend, a true best friend, is the one who can hear the words, "You are doing something unhealthy for your body and your mind, and I hate to watch it—please stop," and be okay. After all, if the words are coming from a true best friend, they should be words to listen to. And remember, a true best friend would not pressure you into doing something you don't want to do. A friend will respect your dreams, boundaries, and beliefs.

CHAPTER FIVE

"Write On" ABOUT FRIENDSHIP

How rare and wonderful is that flash of a moment when we
realize we have discovered a friend.
—William Rotsler, author

Friendship is such a precious and important thing in life that people have been writing about it, singing about it, and cherishing it throughout the ages. This chapter invites you to express yourself when it comes to that special best friend in life. So flex your creative muscles and get writing!

To help you start thinking of what you might want to say about friendship, let's take a look at some quotations from famous people throughout history:

A friend might well be reckoned the masterpiece of nature.
—RALPH WALDO EMERSON, American lecturer, poet, and essayist

If you would win a man to your cause, first convince him that you are his sincere friend.
—ABRAHAM LINCOLN, sixteenth U.S. president

God gives us our relatives; thank God we can choose our friends.
—ETHEL WATTS MUMFORD, twentieth-century American novelist

My best friend is the one who brings out the best in me.
—HENRY FORD, American industrialist

Friendship is a single soul dwelling in two bodies.
—ARISTOTLE, fourth-century B.C.
Greek philosopher and scientist

A faithful friend is a medicine of life.
—PROVERB

I never considered a difference of opinion in politics, in religion, in philosophy, as a cause for withdrawing from a friend.
—THOMAS JEFFERSON, third U.S. president

A friend to all is a friend to none.
—PROVERB

One loyal friend is worth ten thousand relatives.
—EURIPIDES, fifth-century B.C. Greek dramatist

Be slow in choosing a friend, but slower in changing him.
—PROVERB

False friends are worse than open enemies.
—Proverb

In the end, we will remember not the words of our enemies, but the silence of our friends.
—Martin Luther King Jr., civil rights leader, minister

He is a good friend who speaks well of us behind our back.
—Proverb

The way to have a friend is to be one.
—Proverb

We cherish our friends not for their ability to amuse us, but for ours to amuse them.
—Evelyn Waugh, twentieth-century British novelist

Which quote above do you like the most? Which does your best friend like? Think about why you find a certain quote appealing. The authors of these quotes include famous writers, playwrights, politicians, and great leaders. But you don't have to be famous to have something important to say about friendship. Think about something you'd like to say about friendship. How is it important to you? What are some of the most important values a person must have in order to be a true friend? What is the difference between a real friend and a false friend? What are the qualities that true friends have?

In the space below, write your own quotes about friendship. You can even write to us, in care of www.bestfriendshandbook.com, and maybe we'll use your quote on the site!

_____

_____

_____

_____

_____

_____

_____

_____

_____

AS HAPPY AS A CLAM

Remember learning about similes and metaphors in school? Similes are comparative phrases that use "like" or "as." For example, "She is as happy as a clam" or "He is as quiet as a mouse." A metaphor draws a more direct comparison, for example, "Our friendship is an eternal flame" (not using "like" or "as"). Another way to get creative about friendship is to use a simile or a metaphor to describe how you feel. Does your friend make you feel as light as a feather inside? As free as a dolphin? Use your imagination and think of a new way to express your feelings.

My friendship makes me feel _____

_____

_____

_____

When my best friend and I are together, we are as _____ as

_____

You know my best friend and I are around because we're the ones being as

_____ as _____

A POET WHO DOESN'T KNOW IT

Poetry can be very beautiful. Sometimes it can even be a little hard to understand. But poetry is a special way to *express* how you feel.

Not all poetry has to rhyme. Some poetry does, but other poems are free form. Some can be as short as a haiku, those deceptively simple poems from Japan you may have learned about in school. Some poems can be silly. Some can be profound.

Let's get creative with poetry. One simple poem is to take the letters of a person's name and spell out the qualities you think describe them, like this:

Adorable

Loves music

Energetic

Xcellent!

Artistic

Caring

Athletic

Interesting

Talkative

Likable

Intelligent

Never a dull moment

After you compose a "name poem," why not try your hand at a more complicated poem or a silly one? You can use any rhyming pattern or none at all. You could even write a limerick. Limericks are light or humorous poems that go something like this:

> We like pizza with sardines and chips
> Some think that our stomachs do flips
> Our friends scream it's gross
> But we like it the most
> Washed down with cold milk in big sips!

FILL-IN-THE-BLANK FUN

Have you ever played a party game where you have to ask the other person for words like *noun*, *adjective*, etc. Using their words, you fill in the blanks until you end up with an utterly silly story. Fill in the blanks here for your own special, silly story about you and your best friend. Remember, just ask for the adjectives, nouns, etc., but don't read the story until all the blanks are filled in. Have fun!

Me and My Best Friend

My best friend has **[name a color]** _____ hair and **[name a color]** _____ eyes. She is **[name three adjectives]** _____ , _____ , and _____ .

My best friend and I do many fun things together. We like to **[name two verbs]** _____ and _____ . One favorite activity is to have a sleepover. She always arrives with her **[name a color]** _____ **[name an animal]** _____ slippers. We like to eat pizza with **[name a food]** _____ on top. We especially like to drink **[name a liquid]** _____ .

My best friend and I like eating **[name a candy bar]** _____ . Last time we had a sleepover, she ate **[name** a number] _____ !

    My best friend likes **[name a person of the opposite sex you both know]** _____. Last time we had a sleepover, my best friend talked in her sleep and kept saying this person's name over and over. I like **[name another person of the opposite sex you both know]** _____. This person is very **[adjective]** _____ and **[adjective]** _____ .

    My best friend and I will be friends for **[name a number]** _____ years. When we are older, we will each have **[name a number]** _____ children. We will marry **[name two movie stars of the opposite sex]** _____ and _____ and live happily ever after. I will work as a **[name a career]** _____ , and my best friend will work as a **[name a career]** _____ , but no matter what, we'll be best friends!

    Why not design your own fill-in-the-blank? It's easy. You could create a few for your next slumber party. Have fun!!

CHAPTER SIX

Crystal Ball to the Future

The ornament of a house is the friends who frequent it.
—Ralph Waldo Emerson, nineteenth-century American essayist and poet

When you created your friendship time capsule, part of the fun was picturing where you and your best friend will be five years, ten years, twenty years from now. In this chapter, you get to do more of that in a new and exciting way.

Remember when you used to play pretend? Maybe you played house or pretended you were a king or a queen, an astronaut, or a famous entertainer. Did you know that by imagining things in detail you can actually help them come true?

That's right. You can picture your future as you want it to be, and that can help make it a reality. You imagine your dreams becoming real, and you remain positive, optimistic, and focused. The way you do this is by a process called *visualization*.

Now what does all this have to do with your future? Well, visualization can act as a little crystal ball and can help positive things happen to you—it can be a lot of fun, too. Some of the most successful people in the world, famous athletes, politicians, actors and actresses, singers, musicians, terrific teachers, and businesspersons—all practice visualization. They set goals for themselves and visualize what it will take to get there, and this helps them achieve their dreams.

Following are three visualization exercises. Sit down with your best friend and fill in the blanks. Dream great dreams, think of everything you want to accomplish in life, and don't let self-doubt stand in your way. This is a place for YOUR dreams. This is your book, after all, and with your best friend you can combine your creativity to dream big dreams for both of you. Having a dream, and setting it as a goal in life, is how you begin to make your dreams come true.

NUMBER ONE: YOUR CAREER IN THE FUTURE

Fill in the blanks for each of you.

What do you want to be when you grow up?

YOU: _____

YOUR BEST FRIEND: _____

Now fill in some details. For instance, if you want to be a singer, what kind of music do you want to sing? If you want to be a teacher, which grade do you want to teach? If you want to be a doctor, what specialty do you want to practice? Stumped? Don't know what you want to be when you grow up? Have your best friend help you. Maybe he or she can see certain talents in you and make a suggestion. And remember, this book is a kind of journal . . . take some chances and dream big dreams. Part of growing up is changing your mind—maybe even a hundred times. Growing up, Erica always wanted to be a writer, but she also toyed with the idea of being a veterinarian, a psychiatrist, and a reporter. Changing your mind is normal, so don't be afraid to try on a career for size. Right now, Alexa wants to be a concert violinist, and she has been playing the violin since she was four. Maybe she'll change her mind (she doubts it), but it is a lot of fun to picture what that life will be like, traveling and playing her violin in a symphony.

Okay, so now is the time to fill in some details about your future career. Do you have your heart set on one in particular? Do you change your mind often? Do you have many interests, or are you narrowing in on one?

YOU: _____

_____

_____

_____

YOUR BEST FRIEND: _____

_____

_____

_____

Now here's where the visualization comes in. Put on some mellow music and picture your lives in your career scenarios. Picture all the little details. Take a few minutes to do this, and maybe talk afterward about any other little details that came to mind. The idea is to make your future plans as "real" to you as possible. And even though it's fun to picture this with your best friend, it is important to visualize when you're alone, too. This is a valuable tool you can use your entire life!

NUMBER TWO: WHAT WILL MAKE YOU HAPPY + CONTENT IN THE FUTURE?

What makes you happy? Is it having a pet? Sports? Shopping? School? Friendships? Your family? All of the above? Here is where you can picture your life in the future with those things around you that will make you happy. This is a time for you to talk to your best friend about the things that make you happy now and the things you hope and dream about that will make you happy in the future.

Here's a funny story: When Erica was a little girl, she knew having a pet would make her happy. But her mother didn't want a pet. Erica, eight years old, was so desperate for a pet that she dug up earthworms and kept them in jars on the back porch and even named them. Yup, earthworms! She distinctly remembers her mother saying to her,

79

"When you get older and have a house of your own, you can have all the pets you want." And guess what? Erica and Alexa and their family have two dogs, a rabbit, a tank full of fish, a canary, two finches, two doves, three parakeets, and a lovebird! And they'd have more pets if they hadn't run out of room! It's important to keep in mind for this exercise that pets do make Erica happy. So something you visualize making you feel contented in the future could very well end up the way you live your life. Erica feels contented caring for little creatures and petting or walking the dogs. And Alexa cares for her parakeet and nurtures it herself.

What else will make you happy? Do you feel you need to live in the country or the city in order to be happy? Do you want a certain kind of house? Do you want to live near your grandparents or parents? Do you want to travel the world? What places around the world do you want to visit? Or do you intend to remain in your hometown forever? Whatever your dreams are about how you will live your life, now is the time to explore them. Whatever you wish for, write about it here:

YOU: _____

_____

_____

_____

_____

_____

YOUR BEST FRIEND: _____

_____

_____

_____

_____

_____

      Next, after you're done traveling, or maybe at the end of your workday, it's time to come home. What kind of home will that be? A house or an apartment? A farm? A beachfront condo? A place in the mountains where you can ski whenever you want?

YOU: _____

_____

_____

YOUR BEST FRIEND: _____

_____

_____

_____

What else do you need to be content? Do you want to have lots of pets? Do you want to be married and have children? Do you want to stay single? Do you want to learn to speak another language or learn about astronomy and stargaze every night? Think of as many details as you can, from little ones that may seem unimportant to really big ones like marriage and children and other major life decisions. Again, the way visualization works is you're telling your mind and body and soul what your dreams are, and this will help you achieve them. If you can make your dreams real in your mind, it is an important first step to making them real in the future.

YOU: _____

_____

_____

_____

YOUR BEST FRIEND: _____

_____

_____

_____

You've just written about it, now dream it. Shut your eyes and picture this wonderful life you have just imagined for yourself. It *can* come true. Remember, we all control our destiny to some point, and you can make your dreams come true with work and dedication.

Now it's time to be silly. This is a totally fun visualization. What you have to do is picture that you and your best friend are roommates years from now (pick an age when you're just getting out on your own, maybe after college or after you have your first job). Where are you living? Whom are you dating? What do you like to do on the weekends? This time, you can choose scenarios from your wildest dreams. The idea is to have fun. Dating a famous actor and appearing on Broadway every night? On the cover of *People* magazine? Climbing Mount Everest—the first best friend mountain-climbing team to do so? Come on . . . the sky's the limit. Be silly. Be creative. Be wild. Be fun.

Our life together _____

_____

_____

_____

_____

_____

_____

_____

_____

_____

CHAPTER SEVEN
the Friendship Journey

Friendship is a sheltering tree.
—Samuel Taylor Coleridge, British poet

Friendship is a wonderful journey, and we're honored you chose to spend part of that journey with us. We hope you enjoyed making your time capsule, journaling, writing, visualizing, and sharing your dreams. We hope you learned a bit more about your best friend than you knew when you started.

Before we sign off, we want to ask you to remember a few things and hold them in your heart:

- Being a friend is an honor. Make sure you respect and cherish the role you have chosen and always treat your best friend the special way he or she deserves.

- No matter how hard you try to keep things EXACTLY the same, friendships change and grow over time. Hopefully you'll just keep getting closer and closer, but if you do drift apart, remember to always treasure your memories and treat each other with respect.

- Be there for each other in good times and bad. That's part of the job of "best friend."

- Laugh whenever possible. Humor binds us together!

Thanks again for letting us be a part of your friendship. Remember,

Best Friends
FOREVER!

— *Erica* and *Alexa*

P.S. Visit our Web site at www.bestfriendshandbook.com for lots of extra fun.

ABOUT THE AUTHORS

Erica Orloff is a writer and editor. She has been writing since she was a little girl. She lives with her husband and three children—Alexa, Nicholas, and Isabella—in Florida. Together, they take care of two dogs, one rabbit, a tank full of fish, and nine birds!

Alexa Milo is Erica Orloff's twelve-year-old daughter. She enjoys playing the violin and piano and listening to all kinds of music. She also likes to swim, read, and sing. This is Alexa's first book.

Carolyn Fisher is a freelance illustrator who lives in Calgary, Alberta, Canada. She likes to hike and ski in the Rockies with her best friend and husband, Steve.